Minnesota State Board of Immigration

Minnesota

her agricultural resources, commercial advantages, and manufacturing

capabilities - being a concise description of the state of Minnesota, and

the inducements she offers to those seeking homes in a new country

Minnesota State Board of Immigration

Minnesota
her agricultural resources, commercial advantages, and manufacturing capabilities
- being a concise description of the state of Minnesota, and the inducements she
offers to those seeking homes in a new country

ISBN/EAN: 9783337238452

Printed in Europe, USA, Canada, Australia, Japan

Cover: Foto ©Andreas Hilbeck / pixelio.de

More available books at **www.hansebooks.com**

MINNESOTA,

AGRICULTURAL RESOURCES,

Commercial Advantages,

AND

MANUFACTURING CAPABILITIES.

BEING A

CONCISE DESCRIPTION OF THE STATE
OF MINNESOTA, AND THE INDUCE-
MENTS SHE OFFERS TO THOSE
SEEKING HOMES IN A
NEW COUNTRY.

STATE BOARD OF IMMIGRATION:

Governor John S. Pillsbury, President, - - - St. Paul.
Secretary of State J. S. Irgens, - - - St. Paul.
State Treasurer, Wm. Pfaender, - - - - St. Paul.
Clerk of Supreme Court, Samuel H. Nichols, - St. Paul.
Dillon O'Brien, Esq., - - - - - St. Paul.

Address H. H. Young, Secretary of Board.

ST. PAUL, MINN.
H. M. SMYTH & CO., PRINTERS,
1879.

DEDICATION.

TO those desiring to possess homes of their own in a beautiful, healthy and prosperous country, to business men contemplating changes of location, and to all who wish to earn a comfortable maintenance for themselves and families, this pamphlet is respectfully dedicated.

Its purpose is to convey a knowledge of the advantages which the State of Minnesota possesses, and invite all who would escape the exhausting competition and hopeless drudgery of the overcrowded countries of Europe and the eastern portions of our own continent, or the debilitating humid southern atmospheres, to cast their lots with us in this extensive and fertile region, and, aiding in its development, share the rewards it yields so abundantly to intelligent industry.

It is hoped that the following pages will be attentively perused, and the invitation which is here given accepted by many of those who are looking to the West for prospective homes.

MINNESOTA IN 1879.

INTRODUCTION.

The State of Minnesota offers inducements to immigrants which cannot be surpassed and are rarely equalled by any other country on the globe. These comprise excellence of climate, soil and water; agricultural, manufacturing and commercial advantages, and educational facilities; and, in addition to all these, cheap lands! The settler who comes into this State now has not to undergo privations and hardships attendant upon pioneering, nor is he under the necessity of submitting to the inconveniences of frontier life, for there is practically no such thing as frontier in the State, except in the pineries of the extreme north. A glance at the accompanying map will show that it is difficult to locate anywhere (below the line of the Northern Pacific Railway) at the distance of a short day's journey from a railroad, and as these are being annually extended and augmented in numbers, the intervening spaces are continually narrowing, or being afforded facilities by means of branches extending laterally from the main lines. Mills, stores, schools, churches, etc., are met with almost everywhere, and opportunities for social intercourse are at the command of even those in the most sparsely settled neighborhoods.

Notwithstanding this, however, there is still a large proportion of unoccupied land in all parts of the State, except in the older counties near the Mississippi, St. Croix and Minnesota rivers. These water-courses were originally the only channels of communication between Minnesota and the older States, and the early settlements were formed along their banks. Since 1862, however, the building of railways has been prosecuted with marvelous rapidity, and those who have since immigrated hither have located along their lines or proposed routes, thus leaving the intermediate spaces unsettled, although the lands are equally good and often more desirable for agricultural purposes. As the roads were extended, the same course was pursued by the newer arrivals—the government lands within the limits of railroad grants being usually preferred; until to-day the State is belted with settlements, extending from east to west, and one line reaches to its extreme north-west corner. These lines of occupation become narrower and less dense as they recede from the east, but are, for the most part, sufficient for the establishment of schools and societies; and stores, where goods are sold at no greater advance of prices than the cost of additional freight, are found at all the railway stations.   Here, also, the farmer finds a ready market for his grain.

The small squares on the accompanying map represent townships. The lines are uniformly six miles apart, and it is very nearly eight and a half miles diagonally across the townships. Guided by them, it is easy for the reader to calculate the proximity of the railways to any locality between their lines. This season the several extensions indicated by dotted lines on the map will be finished, and probably a branch line built from the Winona and St. Peter road at Tracy to Sioux Falls. These additions will leave very few places in the State destitute of all the railroad facilities they require at present.

The design of this chapter, however, is merely to introduce the subject, leaving the several attractions of the State to be especially treated under appropriate headings, but it is not out of place to add here that the utmost care has been observed throughout, in the preparation of these pages, to avoid exaggeration. It must be borne in mind that this pamphlet is not the production of an individual or company interested in the sale of lands, but a publication issued by authority of the State, after careful revision by its highest officers. While its object is to set forth the inducements which Minnesota offers to immigrants and invite the latter to settle within her borders, those having charge of its publication fully appreciate that, if mutual benefits are to flow from immigration, new settlers must not be attracted by representations which their future experience will not verify. Should they be deceived they may become dissatisfied, and results may follow alike injurious to both themselves and the State. For this reason it has been deemed of utmost moment that no assertion shall find a place in these pages unless it is entirely true.

LOCATION AND AREA.

The State of Minnesota lies between forty-three and a half and forty-nine degrees north latitude, and extends nearly from the ninetieth to the ninety-seventh meridian of longitude west of Washington. Its length north and south is about three hundred and seventy-five miles, and its mean breadth some two hundred and fifty miles. The map which is attached shows its form. Its boundaries enclose an area of 83,530 square miles, or 53,459,840 acres. Of this expanse 50,759,840 acres are land and, (without including that part of Lake Superior which lies within its limits,) 2,700,000 acres are water surface. An idea of its extent may best be formed, perhaps, by comparing it with other countries; for instance, it is greater than the united areas of all the New England States and Maryland; nearly as large as Ohio and Pennsylvania taken together, or as both North and South Carolina, or Tennessee and Mississippi combined. The acreage of arable land already surveyed in this State, (exclusive of the pine and mineral regions,) is as great as the entire area of Illinois.

Compared with European countries, it is larger than the entire island of Great Britain, and has more than two and a half times the area of Ireland. It contains about two-thirds as many square miles as Prussia, and considerably more than the entire German Empire outside of that kingdom. It is about half the size of Sweden, an l two-thirds as extensive as Norway. The idea of its extent may, perhaps, be better conveyed to some minds by remarking that there are seventy-six counties in the State now, and that one of these, St. Louis, has an area of more than 4,000,000 acres, three others exceed 3,000,000 acres, and four others contain more than 1,000,000. A number of others have over 500,000, and very few less than 300,000 acres. Its territory is, in truth, of magnificent extent, and the term "Empire State of the Northwest," sometimes used in reference to it, is not inaptly applied.

GENERAL FEATURES.

Lying in a high northern latitude, at an elevation of from about one thousand to eighteen hundred feet above tide water, and too remote from the great oceans to be perceptibly affected by their influence, Minnesota may justly claim to possess most of the advantages enjoyed by other countries, while exempted from many of their unfavorable peculiarities. Though by no means mountainous, she has many of the characteristics of such regions, and with myriads of lakes scattered over her territory, is almost free from swamps, and entirely clear of their usually attendant miasms. About one-third of her area is covered with timber, yet she deservedly ranks with the prairie States of the Union, and though far in-land vessels may load at her ports, on Lake Superior and the Mississippi, and convey her produce to all parts of the world with only a single trans-fer of cargo. The mighty Mississippi, with its source in her extreme northern districts, while serving her with motive power for innumerable mills and factories, affords her meanwhile the full benefit of its entire navigable channel for purposes of transportation. The Red River of the North connects her with the immense and fertile regions of Manitoba and the Assiniboine and Saskatchewan valleys, and the St. Croix, on her eastern border, provides that portion of her realm with a water outlet for its pro-ducts. The Minnesota river meanwhile furnishes a navigable water-way across the State from west to east and, with the upper Mississippi, gives interior water transportation facilities of several hundred miles in extent.

Besides these natural channels of communication, her territory is inter-sected with a magnificent network of railways, which are being rapidly increased and extended, affording to all parts of the State ample and con-stantly increasing facilities for transportation and constituting, by their exterior connections, means of speedy communication with all other parts of the Union. Every portion of the State is richly endowed with water-power, and the soil in each locality repays abundantly the labors of the agriculturist, except where it covers inexhaustible stores of mineral wealth.

While there is but little flat land in the State, and none that cannot be readily drained, there is no hilly country other than the river bluffs and the mineral regions north of Lake Superior, the surface being everywhere undulating, both in woodlands and prairie. Indeed, it seems hardly possible that a region can be formed more entirely adapted to the uses and conveniences of civilized mankind.

THE SOIL.

Of a region of the extent of Minnesota, it is only possible to treat here of the several features in a general manner, but fortunately there is a remarkable uniformity of soil throughout the State, inasmuch as it is nearly all an alluvial deposit, varying in depth from one to five or more feet. The exceptional district is on the north shore of Lake Superior, where the land is broken and unfit for cultivation. Generally 'this deposit rests directly upon a stratum of clay, and everywhere the alluvion is mixed with sand in sufficient quantities to hold warmth and render it friable and it abounds in organic matter. To the general reader it is far more important to set forth the results of its cultivation than to instruct him as to the elements composing it, for though he may be familiar with the properties and value of all its constituents, he understands that there are conditions of combination'and external circumstances under the influence of which it must be placed in order to produce desirable results. He can only be assured that these exist by knowing what the soil has produced, and instead of consuming space in attempting further to describe its peculiarities, we refer him to the articles upon the several agricultural products of Minnesota, which appear in the pages that follow.

CLIMATE AND TEMPERATURE.

The climate of Minnesota is one of its chief glories, and experience only confirms what has been from time to time hitherto spoken and written in its praise. It is true that the State lies in a high northern latitude, but not more so than Maine and Canada on this continent, and nearly all of Europe in the old world. Christiania, in the southern part of Norway, is in latitude sixty degrees north. Stockholm, Sweden, in fifty-nine, and all of Great Britain and Ireland north of fifty. The German Empire is all north of forty-six degrees. Were latitude alone the index to climate and temperature, Minnesota would compare well with the most favored regions of the earth, but other causes are known to have influence, and the isothermal or climatic zones of the earth are curved irregularly because of peculiarities in the conformation of its surface.

The isothermal zone in which Minnesota is embraced is the same as that of Ohio and Pennsylvania, and so far as temperature is concerned, the climates of these States are somewhat similar. But it ought only to be required to show that the cold here does not prevent the growth, full development, and profitable yielding of cultivated vegetation, and that it can be endured by men and domestic animals with no greater inconvenience or discomfort than it occasions, during the winter seasons, in most countries of the north temperate zone lying above thirty-eight degrees of latitude on this continent, and forty-four in Europe. The magnificent crops of wheat, corn, oats, fruits, vegetables, etc., which are annually grown in this State, and their wide extended reputation for superior quality, are surely sufficient to demonstrate beyond question that the temperature is not detrimental to agricultural success, and the united testimony of its nearly 800,000 inhabitants ought to prove that they experience no excessive discomfort because of the cold.

If further evidence is required, the invalids who flock here annually from all parts of the United States may be referred to. These refugees from death by lingering diseases contracted in the humid climates of more southerly localities, find in the pure, dry atmosphere of Minnesota a panacea for the ills they suffer; and, if the vitality of their systems is not too completely exhausted, they usually recover health upon a few years residence in this State. One who has had such experiences cares little whether the mercury mounts above or sinks below zero. He knows that he can keep himself comfortable with the clothing he has been accustomed to wearing, and that he is free from that sense of numbness and shivering which often caused him so much suffering while in his former home; that the blood courses healthfully through his veins, diffusing warmth and life and filling him with buoyant energy to which he had long been a stranger.

The air here is too attenuated to float the noxious gases so injurious to health, and being always in motion, is purified by constant circulation. Both mankind and animals are benefitted by living in it, and the low annual mean temperature of the climate is due rather to its uniformly cool summer nights than to excessive degrees of cold in winter. And it is largely owing to the coolness of the nights during the warm term that it is so beneficial to invalids, for they are thereby able to obtain refreshing sleep, a blessing which is denied them in hot, suffocating southerly regions. No one need fear the cold of Minnesota who can endure that of Ohio and Pennsylvania, for the mercury sinks at times nearly as low there as it does here, while here the system is in a much better condition to endure the cold.

LENGTH OF SEASONS.

There is no appreciable difference between this country and the middle States of the Union generally in the length of the seasons. Spring commences about the close of March or early in April, and planting is done but little later than in Ohio. Harvest usually commences in July and is continued into August. The early autumnal frosts make their appearance about the first of October, but it is in this month that Indian summer begins, and it frequently lasts from four to six weeks. This is the most delightful of all seasons. The air is cool and balmy, and all nature wears a peculiar aspect of calmness and rest, which is most delightful to the senses. The advent of wintry weather, until which time fall plowing may be continued, takes place about the twentieth of November usually, and the farmer has ample time to prepare his ground for early seeding in the spring. After this the cold increases gradually in severity until winter really sets in about the middle of December. It is not the case, either, that winter is constantly cold, for there are warm intervals throughout its continuance, noticeably so between the middle of January and the middle of February.

WATERS—SUPPLY AND QUALITY.

In the surveyed area of the State there are upwards of 5,000 lakes. Their average extent is about three hundred acres, but a number of them exceed 10,000 and two or three cover respectively about 100,000 acres. Many of them are very deep, and most are filled with fish. Ordinarily their shores are dry and firm down to the waters' edge, except at their out-lets, and the waters clear, cool and pure. The bottoms are commonly sandy or pebbly.

The existence of these lakes is necessarily attended with that of a mul-titude of streams, varying in size from the tiny rivulet fed by a single spring to the majestic Mississippi. Besides this bountiful surface supply of one of mankind's prime necessities, good water is easily reached by digging, in every part of the State.

Inasmuch as the reader has access to the map, and can form a tolerably correct idea of the size of the larger lakes and of the length of the streams by the aid of the township lines, it appears hardly worth while to delay here for the purpose of particularizing, but, as a further help, it may not be uninteresting to remark that Lake Minnetonka contains 16,000 acres; Lake Winnebagoshish, 56,000 acres; Leech Lake, 114,000 acres; and Mille Lacs, 130,000 acres. Red Lake, which is much larger than any other in the State, has not yet been surveyed. The Mississippi, Minnesota, St. Croix and Red Rivers are large navigable streams; and the St. Louis, Big Fork, Red Lake, Wild Rice, Buffalo, Pomme de Terre, Chippewa, Lac qui Parle, Rock, Yellow Medicine, Cottonwood, Des Moines, Blue Earth, Root, Zumbro, Cannon, Rum, Snake, Crow Wing, Crow, Kettle and sev-eral others, are streams of considerable size during even their low water periods; while a thousand, more or less, of others are of sufficient size to make them worthy of note in a less favored country.

ÆSTHETIC FEATURES.

Minnesota affords unparalleled opportunities for building homes amid beautiful scenery, and such considerations are certainly worthy the atten-tion of the immigrant. They contribute largely to the gratification of himself and family, and greatly enhance the value of his farm if he should desire to sell it. It is far more difficult to find locations in the State, however, that are destitute of beautiful surroundings than it is to secure those which possess them in an uncommon degree. The undulating prairies, dotted with lakes and groves and traversed by murmuring streams; the park-like oak openings, with rolling surface and sunny sheets of water shining in the distance; the woodlands and pineries, river bluffs, and even the rugged north shore of Lake Superior, all have their æsthetic attractions, the preference for which must depend upon the tastes of the beholder. Song birds of several varieties are numerous, and, in the proper seasons, the air is filled with the melody of their matin and vesper warblings. The senses of sight, smell and hearing are constantly delighted, and the benign influence which these charms of nature exert is manifested in the sentiments and conduct of people dwelling continually subject to their inspirations. From any given point, a ride of a few miles will convey an excursion, fishing or pic-nic party to a delightful lake, or grove, or stream, for these opportunities of enjoyment abound everywhere.

But it is in winter that Minnesota ministers most graciously to the æsthetic inclinations of mankind. Nothing can be more enchantingly beautiful than many of her winter days. It is at this season of the year that her atmospheric phenomena are most magnificent. No pen or pencil can portray the grandeur of her sunrises, and the mind can only appreciate by observation the brilliancy of her auroras. It is at this season that her skies are bluest and gemmed at night with the brightest stars, and the pure bracing air fits one for the enjoyment of the beauty surrounding him.

CHARACTER OF THE PEOPLE.

The adult population is mostly made up of native-born citizens of other States, with a large per centage of immigrants from Germany, Sweden, Norway, Ireland, England, Scotland and Canada, and fewer numbers of Welsh, Poles, Bohemians, Russians and French. These readily affiliate with each other on acquiring the English language, and prejudices of race and nationality are soon overcome by association. The tone of public sentiment is eminently moral, and a high average degree of intelligence prevails. The importance of educating the young is appreciated by all classes of citizens, and schools are well attended and sustained. All the Christian sects of religion are represented, and the clergy of the State are usually highly educated, liberal-minded and conscientious. Taken altogether, there is hardly a neighborhood in the State that does not afford agreeable social advantages, and strangers are welcomed with generous hospitality.

COMMERCIAL.

The railroads marked on the accompanying map show, better than language can tell, how near every neighborhood in the State is to these lines of transportation. South of the Northern Pacific road there are now but four localities where the distance is more than twenty-five miles, and the extensions proposed to be constructed this season will leave but one. These improvements will, no doubt, continue to keep pace with the future development of the country. Nor are they confined to the interior of the State, but in all directions beyond its borders connect with lines crossing other States and Territories and constitute our local roads parts of a great national system, thus giving the producers of Minnesota whatever benefits are to be derived from having ready access to competitive intermediate and terminal markets.

First, our own Lake Superior port of Duluth is reached by the St. Paul and Duluth road, connecting at St. Paul and Minneapolis with lines traversing the entire southern and western portions of the State; also from St. Paul and the central parts of the State by the branch line of the St. Paul and Pacific, which forms a junction, through the Minnesota Western, with the Northern Pacific at Brainerd in Crow Wing county; and, again, from the western section of the State by the Northern Pacific road. Leading to Milwaukee and Chicago are the West Wisconsin, two lines of the Chicago, Milwaukee and St. Paul, and the Chicago and Northwestern; the Southern Minnesota, likewise, has communication with those cities, and the Green Bay and Winona road affords a route to the third Lake Michigan port. The Minneapolis and St. Louis Railroad, crossing all the intermediate east and west lines running through the country between Minneapolis and St. Paul and its southern terminus, brings these cities in close commercial relationship with that entire fertile region; by the St. Paul and Sioux City and its connections with the Union Pacific we have a direct thoroughfare to the Pacific Coast; and the St. Vincent Extension up the Red River is part of a continuous line to Winnipeg in Manitoba. In short, there are few places in the State from which a person cannot start by the most direct route to travel to any part of the United States or Canada.

Only a few years will probably elapse before the Northern Pacific Railroad, which already affords us commercial intercourse with the mining districts of Montana, will be completed to the Pacific coast in Washington territory; and as the British American road progresses from Thunder bay on Lake Superior, by the way of Winnipeg and the Saskatchewan valley, to British Columbia, it will no doubt be tapped by a line connecting it directly with Duluth, to construct which a company is already formed, and the St. Vincent Extension of the St. Paul and Pacific branch line, together with the Winnipeg road already built, will connect it directly with St. Paul and Minneapolis.

The deepening of the rivers and straits between the great lakes, now only navigable for vessels drawing twelve feet, will soon be sufficient to render the ports of Minnesota on Lake Superior accessible to large seagoing vessels; and the improvement of the channel of the Mississippi, in course of prosecution by the general government, will ere long make its navigation to St. Paul practicable for large class steamboats during the entire season.

With all these advantages of external communication, and with her already immense interior facilities of transportation by land and water, Minnesota ought, and it would seem must, place herself in the first rank amongst the commercial States of the Union within a very few years.

A COMMERCIAL THOROUGHFARE.

The exterior transportation facilities described in the foregoing article will do more than afford outlets for the products of Minnesota. By their means, in conjunction with lines traversing other States, she will become a general thoroughfare of commerce and travel. In winter, whatever transportation flows eastward from the western portions of Britsih America, or by way of the Northern Pacific Railroad, including through freight and travel from China and Japan, will be diverted from its direct course, in consequence of the suspension of lake navigation, and seek the continuation of its journey by railroad lines running from St. Paul eastward. And in summer seasons much of the travel eastward by the Union Pacific and its auxiliary lines, will bend northward through Minnesota to enjoy the luxury of water transportation from Duluth. All this passing freight and travel will augment the commercial importance of this State, and many of the thousands of tourists who annually pass over the great thoroughfares of the country, attracted by the delightful climate, beautiful scenery and excellent opportunities for hunting and fishing, will stop here for recreation. Thus the peculiarities of the situation of the State will not only tend to add to her commerce, but indirectly contribute to enhance the prices of her products generally in her home markets and increase the value of her real estate.

RAILROADS IN THE STATE.

In describing the commercial facilities enough has been said to give an intelligent idea of the capacities for transportation which the present railroads of Minnesota afford, but it may not be amiss to speak briefly of their building and of the new roads and extensions already in contemplation. The first road in the State was built in 1862. It was only ten miles long. A mere initial step. From that time on the work has progressed rapidly, except during the four years of general business depression from 1873 to 1876 inclusive. In short, nearly the entire railway system of the State, having a total length of 2,608 miles, is the work of twelve years, and the question suggests itself : with the increased opportunities now afforded for transporting ties and rails, what time will be required to build the new roads already projected ? These are : extensions of the Southern Minnesota from Jackson to the State line in Lincoln county, of the Hastings and Dakota from Montevideo to the head of Big Stone Lake, of the St. Vincent Extension of the Branch Line of the St. Paul and Pacific to connect at or near Barnesville with that part of the line already built from Breckenridge to St. Vincent. New roads are proposed as follows : from Fergus Falls in Otter Tail county, to tap the Northern Pacific at Verndale, in Wadena county ; from Anoka to Spencer Brook in Isanti county, to be continued ultimately to the line of the Northern Pacific; from Red Wing in Goodhue county to Faribault ; from the line of the Winona and St. Peter at Tracy to Sioux Falls, in Dakota ; a branch of the Sioux City road from Lake Crystal to Blue Earth City in Faribault county; and a branch of the St. Paul and Duluth from White

Bear Lake to Taylor's Falls in Chisago county. All of these will probably be built this season, and there are, besides, a number of other roads projected, the routes, etc., of which are less definitely determined upon.

It is proper to add here that a number of these railroad companies still have considerable bodies of unoccupied lands to sell. The terms are exceedingly liberal in every instance, and great credit is due the companies for the earnest efforts they are putting forth to attract immigration. They not only sell their lands on advantageous terms, but transport all those who go to view the lands and such as are immigrating to settle upon them at cheap rates of fare for themselves and of freight for the carrying of their effects. They, likewise, operate their roads, both in conveying supplies to and shipping produce from the remote counties, so as best to promote the interests of the settlers in those regions, providing them with every facility enjoyed by the more densely populated portions of the State, at less than proportionate cost for transportation.

MANUFACTURING.

No State in the Union is richer than Minnesota in capabilities of manufacturing. At Minneapolis, the St. Anthony falls of the Mississippi river affords a water power of magnificent available capacity. It is already utilized by nineteen flouring mills with an aggregate of 220 run of stone and capacity for the manufacture of about 1,650,000 bbls. of flour per year; by twenty saw and shingle mills, with eighteen gang, twenty-five double circular and a number of smaller saws; and by manufactories of cotton and wool, farm machinery, etc. The St. Croix river, above Stillwater, in Washington county, and especially in the vicinity of Taylor's Falls, in Chisago county, affords a series of superb water powers, in the aggregate equalling, if not surpassing, that of St. Anthony Falls. These are partially improved now in running flouring and saw-mills and other machinery, and with the rapidly increasing railroad facilities which are being afforded that section of the State, and the constant large additions made to its population annually, they will no doubt be much more extensively employed in the early future. At Fergus Falls, on Red River, is another extraordinary power, computed to be equal to over 20,000 horse-power, all of which can be easily and cheaply made available. It is not yet improved to any considerable extent, but will be during the current season. A good deal of flour is already manufactured there for home consumption and to supply the Manitoba market.

At Granite Falls on the upper Minnesota river, in Yellow Medicine county, is still another of over twelve thousand horse-power capacity, improved partially, there being two flouring mills in operation there. Another power of extraordinary capacity, and easily and entirely made available, is found on the St. Louis river, near Thomson, in Carlton county. This is about to be improved somewhat extensively for sawing lumber, as it is adjacent to an extensive pine region.

Three of the above, viz.: that at Minneapolis, that on the St. Croix, and that on the St. Louis river, justly deserve to be called gigantic powers, while the others already mentioned, and one at Sauk Rapids in Stearns county, another on the Cottonwood in Brown county, and, perhaps, a dozen more in as many different localities, are very extensive and valuable powers. Most of these are wholly unimproved, and probably the full capacity of none is yet made available. Houston county has a fine power on Root river of very considerable capacity, and there are several others on that stream in that and Fillmore counties. On the Zumbro river there are four or five extensive powers, and on the Cannon some eight or ten Indeed, there are several hundred streams scattered all over the State which afford four or five times the water power needed for the districts adjacent to them. On looking over the Statistical Report for 1878, it is found that sixty-three counties reported 452 flour mills. These probably manufacture about 5,500,000 barrels per year. All but about 500,000 barrels of this, which is the product of steam mills, is the result of the water-power of the State now improved, and besides this there is an immense manufacture of lumber accomplished by the same agency, and a good many other factories derive their motion from this source; yet hardly one-twentieth of the capacity of the water-power of the State is yet made available. Every county in the State it is believed has more or less available water-power within its borders.

This widely diffused and immense mechanical force gives ample opportunity for Minnesota to send all the products of her fields, flocks, forests and mines to market in their prepared conditions, thereby avoiding expense of transportation on the refuse portions, saving for her own use those parts which are not profitably marketable, and giving employment to thousands of her citizens in the mechanical departments of industry, thus securing to the State the greatest possible share of the profits accruing from her products.

MINNESOTA FLOUR.

In the foregoing article on the manufacturing capabilities of the State, incidental mention is made of the already extensive milling interests. No data is obtainable at the moment from which to derive an approximate idea of the amount invested in this single business, but it is necessarily very large, for a number of our Minnesota mills are the finest in the world. Those at Minneapolis are especially noticeable, and are visited by persons who come here from the eastern States as objects particularly worthy of curiosity. At Stillwater, St. Paul, Red Wing, Cannon Falls, Northfield and Lanesboro, and on the Zumbro river, and at Sauk Centre, Mankato, Fergus Falls, and several other points, are others less extensive but still of considerable dimensions and expensive construction, and in most instances supplied with all the recently improved machinery and apparatus for the manufacture of the best description of flour. The flour manufactured of Minnesota wheat, and by mills in this State, has for years ranked highest in the eastern and foreign markets, and commanded the best prices, and for the past two or three years has been in especial demand for shipment to Europe. About a year ago orders began to be received by the millers here directly from foreign dealers, for the double purpose of making sure of obtaining the flour desired and saving the additional expense of commissions and forwarding charges at eastern ports. This trade has grown rapidly, Minneapolis alone having shipped last year 109,183 barrels direct to foreign ports, and several other mills considerable quantities, and it continues to increase, thus augmenting the ability of the millers to pay higher prices for the wheat, and in that way contributing to benefit the agriculturalists of the State. From the satisfaction which has so far been given to both shippers and receivers there is no doubt but that this direct trade will continue to grow until it covers the entire quantity of Minnesota flour sent to Europe.

MANUFACTURES OF WOOD.

Owing to the circumstance that the laws of the State do not impose upon any of the local officers the duty of gathering manufacturing statistics, leaving the State Statistician dependent upon voluntary contributions for this kind of information, it follows that the reports are necessarily incomplete. Yet, notwithstanding this, the aggregated showing in the report for last year is very considerable. Manufactories of wood are reported in fifty-two counties, and number 715 establishments. These embrace 207 sawmills, forty-eight counties containing one or more; 352 wagon and carriage factories, 33 planing mills, 54 cooper shops, 26 shops for the manufacture of blinds, sash and doors, 14 furniture factories, 20 establishments for making agricultural machinery, and five others for making packing boxes, show-cases, and laths and shingles. A considerable number of these establishments are quite large, employing a good many hands and heavy investments of capital, and the others are continually increasing their extent and facilities, while additions to their number are made every season. The possession of material and facilities for its profitable manufacture has already placed Minnesota in the category of States which export manufactures of wood, and she is gradually assuming a higher position in that list with the opening of the newer regions west and northwest, besides supplying the rapidly increasing home demand consequent upon the annual influx of new settlers within her own borders

SUGAR MAKING AND REFINING.

The manufacturing and refining of syrup and sugar from Amber Cane, which has heretofore been confined to farmers growing the cane, is about to be made an especial department of industry in this State The uniform testimony of Southern sugar refiners as to excellence of the products of this cane, and the analysis of the raw sugar made by the chemist of the national agricultural bureau in Washington, have led enterprising capitalists here to regard it as of utmost importance that facilities shall be provided in the State for manufacturing and refining it, under all the advantages of improved appliances and scientific skill, and a company is now about organizing in Faribault, Rice county, to build, furnish and operate such factory and refinery. Should success attend their efforts, the example will, no doubt, be followed, and it may be confidently expected that the business will shortly grow into importance. Both sugar and syrup, produced in this State, have been sent hence to St. Louis to be refined, and the experiments have been entirely successful. The products were pronounced fully equal to the syrups and sugars obtained from canes of Louisiana and Cuba. The chemist of the agricultural bureau gave the following as the analysis of the Amber Cane sugar above alluded to, viz.:

Cane Sugar (saccharose) 88.8934
Grape Sugar (glucose) 5.6100
Water (by drying at 110 deg. C.) 5.5250

Analyses made by other chemists confirm this, all of them giving the saccharine element as comprising more than 87 per cent., and thus showing the product to equal the cane sugar in sweetening power and wholesomeness.

CLAYS, SANDS, LIME, STONE, &c.

Clays are found in abundance in many localities, and they are generally of excellent quality. Fifteen counties report brick-yards in their territories, and the aggregate number of these is thirty in the entire State. Several of them are, however, quite extensive, and the total of manufactures in this line is an item of considerable importance. In Red Wing, Goodhue county, and New Ulm, Brown county, there are extensive potteries where a very superior quality of stone-ware is manufactured. This is commonly preferred to the ware sent here from abroad, because of the fineness of the clay used. An excellent quality of fire-brick is also made at the same factories. Near the bed whence the clay used in Red Wing is taken there is an extensive deposit of much finer quality, suitable for the manufacture of queensware of a higher than average standard. There are a number of clay-beds elsewhere in the State, only awaiting the demand for their development, to furnish material for other factories and make this an important branch of industry.

Limestone is found in various neighborhoods, and a large quantity of lime is manufactured annually both for home consumption and exportation. The quarrying of both limestone and granite for building purposes is, also, already an important industry in a number of localities, in the vicinity of the Mississippi and Minnesota rivers. Rich quarries of granite of excellent quality are found on the Mississippi river near Sauk Rapids, and likewise along the upper Minnesota river, and in the Lake Superior region; and an excellent description of durable building stone is quarried from the bluffs in the vicinity of Lake Pepin, on the Mississippi, and at Kasota, on the Minnesota river. The demand for this kind of material for building purposes must be the means of affording employment for a good many persons in the not distant future.

In localities along the Mississippi bluffs immense deposits of white sand are, likewise, found. This has been tested and found very superior for the manufacture of glass, for which purpose considerable quantities of it have been already exported. There are likewise several quarries of a fine quality of slate in the State.

Iron ore of extraordinarily good quality, which it is claimed yields a metal equal to the best Swedish iron, and copper ore of exceeding richness, are found in almost inexhaustible quantities in the region north of Lake Superior. Extremely valuable specimens of silver ore have likewise been obtained in that locality. There is little room for doubting that this will prove one of the most profitable mining districts in the world, when the metallic treasures which lie buried beneath its rugged surface are more fully developed.

NEWSPAPERS AND PRINTING.

There are very few counties in Minnesota in which no newspaper is published; most of them have two, and several have more than two. Among the country newspapers are a score, at least, of large, well-conducted, first-class journals. There are five dailies in the State, all enterprising and ably managed, and one, the Pioneer-Press, compares well with the large dailies of eastern cities, and has a circulation ranking fourteenth among the newspapers of the United States. Well appointed job printing offices are found in all the large towns, and there are besides engraving, lithographing and stereotyping establishments, and one type-foundry.

OTHER MANUFACTURES.

Besides the foregoing there are a variety of other manufactories in operation in the State, consuming material produced within its limits, but generally these are undeveloped industries, and are only alluded to here as serving to illustrate the capabilities of the State in this direction. Amongst these is a large paper mill at Minneapolis, which supplies much of the paper used in the State, besides exporting a considerable proportion of its products. There are, also, fifty-six cigar factories, which work up, in part, the tobacco grown here, together with imported material; and sixty-eight breweries consume a large quantity of the barley produced in the State. A number of factories of leather are, likewise, in operation, and a considerable share of the stock they use is taken from cattle raised here and is tanned in the State. Recently an important business has sprung up in the canning and preserving of fruits and berries grown in the State. Some of the railroad companies are making their cars here, and in Minneapolis, St. Paul, and several other cities, stationary and portable steam engines, equal to those made anywhere, are being manufactured, and a considerable proportion of these are exported. Besides the factories for materials produced here, it will thus be seen that a large amount of capital is employed in the manufacture within the State of materials produced elsewhere, so that Minnesota's manufacturing interests are already of significant proportions.

AGRICULTURAL.

It is from no lack of appreciation of its primary importance that this branch of the subject follows those of manufactures and commerce, but as the agricultural resources of a country are of greatest moment, it was thought expedient to place the other topics more prominently before the reader, in order to insure his attention as well to the facts that this State possesses manufacturing and commercial facilities, which are partially developed and are keeping pace with the extension of her agricultural industries. In treating of the advantages she offers to the agriculturist it is deemed useless to theorize, because the opportunity of summing up results and making just comparisons are at hand, and thus the actual evidence may be presented. Generally the comparisons are made with Ohio, for the reason that the excellences of that State as an agricultural region are widely known, its fertility and careful tillage will not be disputed, and its statistics of agriculture are carefully prepared and entirely reliable.

WHEAT—ITS YIELD AND GRADE.

Wheat is the staple product of Minnesota, not because it is the only grain crop that will mature, nor even for the reason that it is surer and its yield more bountiful, but simply because it always sells readily for cash. Whether the crop is scant or full the farmer is safe in calculating his wheat as so much ready money as soon as he can get it in the market, and it usually brings a remunerative price. This is why the agriculturists of Minnesota have applied themselves mainly to the cultivation of wheat, and thus won for the State the deserved and almost world-wide reputation of producing wheat of a better quality than that grown in any other part of the United States, if not of the world. It is exceedingly rich in nutritive elements, and the flour made from it always commands the highest prices.

The average yield of wheat in this State ranges from about sixteen to twenty bushels per acre, and when, in connection with this statement, it is remembered that the area upon which it is grown includes 1,850,000 acres, scattered over sixty-eight counties, extending about two hundred and sixty miles east and west, and two hundred and eighty north and south, the magnitude of the yield can be more fairly appreciated. It is rarely, if ever, that a season passes without more or less injury to crops resulting from local drouths, storms or other causes in a region so extensive, and it must always be the case that amongst sixty-odd thousand farmers there are a good many who are negligent in tilling their lands and taking care of their produce. When a district of such immense extent shows an average yield of even twelve bushels per acre, the circumstance merits especial mention.

2

In 1877 the average was nineteen and a half bushels per acre. In fourteen counties that season it exceeded twenty bushels. In 1868, 1869, 1872,
1873, and 1875 the general average of the State was more than seventeen
bushels. Another circumstance in connection with cultivating wheat in
this State deserves remark here, that is : the ability of the land to produce
a good crop does not appear to be impaired by continuous cultivation.
The farmers of the older counties have continued to grow wheat on the
same land year after year, without rest, and without the application of
fertilizers, and still the average is well maintained. Grouping the averages of the six years from 1866 to 1871 inclusive, and we discover that the
mean average per acre for each season was 15.34 bushels. Pursuing the
same course with the interval from 1872 to 1877 inclusive, gives us a mean
average or 15.33 bushels. A difference of just one one-hundredth part of
a bushel, yet the latter period included 1876, when the crop of the State
was reduced to its lowest known average. This result is not due to the
continual additions of new lands to the wheat producing area either, as
the following exhibit of the averages of some of the oldest counties in
1877 will show, viz.:

Carver	24.60	Olmsted	20.12
Dakota	17.48	Ramsey	19.24
Dodge	21.45	Rice	23.05
Fillmore	17.81	Scott	21.85
Freeborn	22.29	Steele	23.73
Goodhue	21.58	Wabasha	18.63
Hennepin	20.50	Washington	19.01
LeSueur	21.51	Winona	17.59

Polk was the only new county that made a remarkable showing that
season, its average being 25.19 bushels per acre ! As compared with Iowa,
Illinois and Ohio, the Minnesota average is found to be considerably in excess, whether taken for a single season or for a term of several years, and
its wheat has the further advantage of having a higher grade and greater
money value. On page 503 of the Ohio Statistics for 1877, it is stated that
the "average number of bushels of wheat to the acre in twenty-seven
years is 11.61," and according to the report of the U. S. Commissioner of
Agriculture for 1877, the average yield for that year in Ohio was 15 bus.,
Indiana 14.5 bus., Illinois 16.5 bus., Wisconsin 15 bus., Iowa 14.5 bus.,
Missouri 14 bus., Kansas 13.5 bus., Nebraska 15 bus., California 9.5 bus.;
while Minnesota's yield according to the same authority was 18.5 bushels
per acre !
    The total yield of wheat in this State in 1877 is stated by Hon. J. P.
Jacobson, State Statistician, to have been 32,280,637 bushels by weight of
sixty pounds to the bushel ! There can be no doubt but that this is one
of the greatest wheat-growing regions in the world, and as it is not likely
that the assertion will be contradicted, it seems hardly worth while to
dwell longer upon this theme. If doubt of the statement should exist in
any mind, reference for its confirmation may be made to reports of the U.
S. Agricultural Bureau, and to the statistics published by the several
wheat-producing States. There might be added here a great many well-
authenticated instances of extraordinary yields, occurring in every county

and almost every season, but it is considered inexpedient to publish them, as the Board prefers that the reputation of the State for fertility shall depend upon general results as found in official records, which cannot be disputed.

THE CORN CROP.

Corn has been grown in this State since its earliest settlement, and it matures well and yields abundantly almost every season. In 1867 the area devoted to its culture was 162,722 acres, and in 1877 it had increased to 388,708 acres. The crop of the latter year was much below the usual yield, but even then the average per acre exceeded 28¼ bus. For eight years, embracing the period from 1867 to 1874 inclusive, the average was 32½ bus. per acre, and for the same period in Ohio the average yield was 35⅜ bus. per acre. The largest yields during any year of that period were, in Minnesota, 37⅓ bus. and in Ohio, 40 5-6 bus.; and the lowest 28⅔ bus. in Minnesota and 28⅓ bus. in Ohio. This period includes three years of extraordinary yield in Ohio and only one of uncommon yield in Minnesota. When it is remembered that corn is the staple crop of Ohio, and that particular attention is paid to its cultivation, the acreage devoted to it being more than twice as much as that of wheat; while in Minnesota it is the third crop in importance, having only about one-fifth the acreage that is devoted to wheat and considerably less than that used for oats, it must be admitted that the above is an extraordinarily good showing. The comparison is made, too, with one of the very best and most carefully cultivated corn states of the Union.

THE OAT CROP.

The oats grown in Minnesota are generally heavy and contain an unusual proportion of nutritive constituents. They are held in high esteem for the manufacture of oatmeal. In 1877 the quantity produced was 13,819,630 bus., an average of about 39¼ bus. per acre; and the lowest average yield for the nine years preceding was 28⅔ bus. per acre; the highest being 37½ bus. During the same years in Ohio the lowest average was 22 bus. per acre, and the highest 32⅔ bus., showing that Minnesota is far ahead in the matter of producing oats.

RYE, BARLEY AND BUCKWHEAT.

The yield of rye in this State since 1867 has not fallen below an average per acre of 12¼ bus. nor exceeded 19 bus.; the general average has been about 16 bus. In Ohio during the same interval the lowest average was 9¼ bus. and the highest 11¾ bus., the mean average being about 10⅓ bus. During the same interval barley has ranged in Minnesota from an average of 18⅞ to 30¼ bus., with a mean average of 26 bus., and the quality very superior. The barley of this State is renowned in the markets for its weight, freedom from rust and mature development. In Ohio in the same time the range was for barley from 12⅓ to 26⅔ bus., the mean average being 20⅔ bus. Take Buckwheat in the same period, and we have as the extremes in Minnesota 7¼ and 16⅞ bus., and a mean average of 13¼ bus.; and in Ohio 7⅔ and 12 bus. are the extremes of annual averages and 10¼ bus. the mean. Thus it seems that in all these products Minnesota is ahead of Ohio, notwithstanding the less systematic and careful cultivation arising from her newness.

TIMOTHY, CLOVER, FLAX AND HEMP.

Of tame hay the yields per acre in Ohio and Minnesota are nearly the same. That of Ohio being 1 13-100 tons, and of Minnesota 1 18-100 tons. The cultivation of clover has not, until quite recently, attracted attention here, and there is no data at hand for instituting comparisons. The yield is pronounced by Minnesota farmers to be large. No report is made of the flax fiber grown in Minnesota, but the seed produced is 7 36-100 bus. per acre, and in Ohio 6 9-10 bus., an excess of 46-100 bus. in favor of this State. Both flax and hemp grow well here, and the fibers are excellent, and in the future their cultivation and manufacture will, no doubt, become an important source of wealth to the State.

WILD GRASSES.

The wild grasses of this State are famous for the nourishment they contain. They not only afford rich and ample pasturage, upon which horses, cattle and sheep thrive well, but also make an excellent quality of hay. Many farmers prefer them to timothy for the latter purpose. Three varieties, the buffalo and herd grass and blue joint, after the ground has been mowed over a few times, become fine and succulent and cure very nicely, and even the coarsest variety of slough grass is similarly affected, though its improvement is not so marked. Cattle subsist during the winter on hay of this latter description, and keep in good order if properly sheltered.

FRUITS AND BERRIES.

Minnesota was long ago famous for its wild crab apples, plums, blackberries, strawberries and grapes. These were abundant all over the State, and the qualities were generally excellent. No more delicious wild plums and strawberries are found anywhere, and when improved by cultivation these excel many of the tame varieties. The wild grapes abound most on the bottom lands of creeks and rivers. A choice quality of wine is frequently made from them. Some varieties of the wild crab-apples were formerly used for preserving, but the introduction of tame fruits has obviated the necessity for resorting to them now-a-days. The existence of such wild fruits and berries was, of itself, evidence to some minds that tame fruits, of similar varieties, would grow here, and experiments for their introduction were accordingly made. Tame grapes, plums, crab-apples, strawberries, raspberries, currants and gooseberries were successfully experimented with from the start, but considerable difficulty attended the earlier efforts to introduce the standard apples, and after several failures, those who undertook it became discouraged. It was remembered, however, that similar disappointments attended the introduction of apple-culture into Michigan, now one of the greatest apple-producing States in the Union, and this encouraged Minnesota agriculturists to persevere in their endeavors, and the consequence is that last year there were 203,493 apple trees in bearing in this State, and 1,219,324 growing; and the year before (1877) 15,736 bus. of apples were grown in the State. No report of the quantity of apples raised last year has yet been made by the county assessors. Most of the apples raised were of handsome appearance and excellent flavor, and were preserved through the winter without difficulty.

Tame strawberries were grown in fifty counties, and 203,024 quarts are reported to have been picked last year. These include all the popular varieties known in the Middle States. Fifty-one counties reported bearing grape vines last year, and a total number of 40,743 vines. In 1877 there were 101,973 lbs. of grapes grown in the State. Of the varieties of grapes grown here the most common are the Isabella, Concord and Delaware, and they are certainly luscious fruit. No report is given in the statistics of the State of the cultivated raspberries, blackberries, currants, gooseberries, plums, etc., but they abound everywhere, the yield is prolific and the quality unexcelled. In short, it may be relied upon that there need be no greater scarcity of fruit, both large and small, in Minnesota than in the Middle States generally.

BEES AND HONEY.

Bees and honey are natural products of Minnesota. Wild bees were found here in great plenty when the State was settled, and they thrive well when domesticated. A great many swarms of Italian bees have also been brought here and are found to be easily kept through the winter. There were reported to be 10,835 hives here in 1877, and their produce was 213,768 lbs. of honey. This does not include a great many hives kept in the cities.

GARDEN VEGETABLES AND MELONS.

All the usual varieties of garden vegetables cultivated in the Middle States of the Union are grown here with equal facility, and mature about as early. Root vegetables especially flourish in this soil, and finer potatoes, beets, parsnips, carrots, salsify, radishes, onions, etc., are not raised anywhere; and the water-melons, musk-melons and cantelopes of Minnesota bid fair to become as famous as those of New Jersey used to be. Squashes and pumpkins attain enormous size and are richly flavored; and no better or larger tomatoes are grown anywhere. Cabbage, lettuce, spinach, endives, etc., grow rapidly and are tender and succulent. No finer beans and peas can be grown than those produced here.

MAPLE SUGAR AND SYRUP.

The fact that maple sugar and syrup were manufactured in thirty-six counties last year, shows that maple timber is pretty generally scattered through the State, and as the quantities made are respectively 13,588 gallons of syrup and 52,723 lbs. of sugar, that that variety of forest tree is somewhat abundant. There are maple trees in sufficient quantities for the manufacture of these products in several other counties, but if any was made in them it was not reported. In more than half the counties of the State maple syrup and sugar are manufactured every year.

TOBACCO.

Tobacco is grown in fifty-nine counties, and in 1877 there were 38,839 lbs. raised. This ought to be accepted as sufficient evidence of the length of the growing season, for it is well-known that this plant matures slowly.

AMBER CANE.

The earlier experiments in the manufacture of syrup and sugar from the sorghum cane were unsuccessful in this State, as they were in the northern States of the Union generally. This was partly because the plants would not fully mature, and partly from the crude and imperfect appliances and machinery used in the manufacture of its products. A few years since, however, two enterprising agriculturists of the State, who had given the subject a good deal of attention, procured a variety of cane known as "Early Amber," and since its introduction the efforts in this branch of industry have resulted in the realization of the most sanguine hopes. Proper machinery has recently been obtained for expressing the juice and manufacturing it, and syrup and sugar of very superior quality are now made at their own homes by a large number of our farmers, at comparatively small cost. According to the Statistics of 1878, there was more or less made in fifty counties. Two thousand two hundred acres of cane were grown, and the average yield of syrup was 63.07 gallons per acre. This, however, is much less than might have been obtained had all the farmers who engaged in the manufacture supplied themselves with proper machinery. In those counties where suitable appliances were generally used the yield was from one hundred to one hundred and forty-five gallons per acre. The fact that similar success has not been achieved in other northern States would seem to indicate that Minnesota is peculiarly adapted to the cultivation of Amber Cane.

FOREST TREE CULTURE—FUEL.

Early in the settlement of the State, those who had made homes on the prairies frequently planted about their dwellings and stabling groves of white willow, white maple, cottonwoods, linden and other fast growing trees as a means of shelter from the winds, and in 1873 the officers of the St. Paul and Pacific Railroad Company resorted to a similar expedient to prevent the drifting snows filling the cuts along the line of their road. This gave an impulse to the general culture of forest trees in the prairie districts, and mainly through the instrumentality of the delegation from this State, Congress, in 1873, passed a law for the encouragement of forest tree planting. This has since been amended until it is now efficient to promote this important purpose. In his inaugural message, Gov. Pillsbury suggested that the State likewise lend its assistance to this work by seconding the efforts of the State Forestry Association, an organization formed chiefly through the efforts of its present Secretary, Hon. L. B. Hodges, and the legislature accordingly made a generous appropriation to be distributed by the Association in the shape of premiums. Since then the work of forest-tree planting has made rapid progress, and the results will soon be available for fuel supply, as the groves already are for shelter and scenery.

Aside from this prospective source, the native forests of the State and the adjacent coal-fields of Iowa are ample to satisfy the demand for fuel for many years to come, and the railroad companies, being interested in the early settlement of all parts of the State, that the business of their roads may be thereby increased, are transporting fuel cheaply, so that it can be sold at reasonable prices in the most distant prairie counties. But there is really no portion of the State where enough timber for fuel is not accessible without any very serious inconvenience, even if these favoring circumstances did not exist.

STOCK RAISING.

The richness and abundance of the native grasses and the wide ranges of free pasturage in Minnesota naturally attracted the attention of cattle growers at an early day, and experiments in every instance proved remarkably successful. It was found that the pasturage frequently continued fair until about the middle of November, and in the spring the grass grew rapidly, so that the feeding season was but little, if any, longer than in Illinois or Missouri, and there was no more necessity for grain feeding than in districts further south. This success has led many persons to engage in raising cattle, and the business has already become important, involving in the aggregate a large investment of capital. A gentleman formerly engaged in stock raising in Texas, and afterwards in Kansas, who is now located in Polk county in this State, says that he had no difficulty whatever in wintering his herd during the season that has just passed, and that the cattle are in better condition this spring than was usual in the other localities named. He fed no grain nor has his cattle had extra care, being provided only with shelters made of poles and closed in and covered with straw.

He says that the dryness of the atmosphere and absence of cold rains, mud, sleet and continually varying temperatures more than compensate for the severer cold experienced here ; that the cattle's hair grows enough thicker to protect them and that they are not so liable to become chilled. Again, the quickly grown grasses of this country, cured without exposure to rains and successive falls of dew, retain all their nutritious juices and make stronger and more palatable hay. The extensive natural meadows furnish thousands of tons of this hay, to be had for the cutting and curing, and afford an ample supply of winter feed at little cost.

The cattle contract none of the diseases here incidental to damper climates, and their better health saves the heavy losses which southern stock raisers annually suffer. Besides the common cattle raised here for beef, finer herds of Durhams, Jerseys Ayrshires, Galloways, Herefords, Devons, etc., cannot be found anywhere.

DAIRY FARMING.

The ease and inexpensiveness with which cattle are taken care of and their superb general health, added to the advantages which the cool summer nights of this region afford for preserving milk, has induced a good many of our enterprising farmers to engage in dairy farming. In 1877 there were 200,379 milch cows kept in the State, and 13,433,195 lbs. of butter and 829,075 lbs. of cheese were made. When the proper means are used and the abundant facilities systematically utilized, it is claimed that dairy farming pays better than any other department of agricultural industry. There are forty-six cheese factories in operation in the State and a number of extensive butter making establishments. In 1878 there was an increase of 13,500 milch cows over the number of the preceding year. Much of the butter made in the regular dairy establishments here is shipped to eastern markets and sold for the highest prices, and cheese from Minnesota factories meets with ready sale and the best prices in the markets of England.

SHEEP AND WOOL.

The same causes which make Minnesota an excellent country for raising neat cattle also adapt it for growing sheep and wool. The feed is abundant in quantity, superior in quality and procured cheaply. Sheep require to be cared for in winter, and sheds with high roofs and good ventilation are necessary for the best condition of the flocks. They are not liable to foot-rot, catarrhal affections, and various other ailments as in moister climates; their wool is heavier and grows thicker and of finer fibre because of the greater warmth required in this natural covering in the regularly cold winters of this latitude. There is but little danger from wolves, as the bounties paid by the State for their destruction have led to their becoming very scarce and shy, except in heavily timbered districts. Dogs are their most dangerous foes, and in respect to the numbers of these Minnesota is no worse off than older states. There are a great many fine blooded sheep in the State. In 1878 there were 173,269 sheep, and 645,156 lbs. of wool were sheared. On account of the unusually warm weather of the preceding winter the clip was much lighter than ordinarily that year.

HOGS.

The number of hogs raised in the State last year was 217,183, and the success attending this business is leading to its large annual increase. Hogs thrive well, fatten easily, and require no extra care whatever. Of late a good deal of attention has been paid to improving the stock and on most of the farms the drove of hogs attracts the visitor's attention. Minnesota farmers appear to have accepted the conviction that it is as cheap to feed the best as the worst animals, while the profit is much greater, and therefore, the improved breeds are the universal favorites.

HORSES.

Horses appear to become hardier and more capable of endurance in this climate, even when brought here from countries further south after their maturity, and those raised here are certainly much better than the average from other States. In part this is due, no doubt, to the care that has been taken in introducing the best stock, but it is also largely owing to the healthfulness of the climate and the superior nutritive properties of the feed. There are 204,983 horses in the State, and amongst them is a larger proportion of perfectly healthy, handsome animals than is to be seen elsewhere, and they always meet with ready sale and bring good prices when shipped to eastern markets.

BEEF, MUTTON AND PORK.

Mr. George Baihly, an experienced butcher of Rochester, Minnesota, who has followed the business for more than twenty years here, after an experience of fifteen years in Ohio and Indiana, declares that the meats of animals raised here are decidedly superior to those of the two other localities named, and the experienced butchers of the State confirm this assertion. The animals slaughtered are found to be free from diseases of liver, kidneys, or intestines; the flesh is firm and solid and abounding in natural juices. This is true of all the domestic animals whose meats are used for food. There were never any signs of trichina discovered in Minnesota hogs, and the bacon made from them is dense without being dry, and deliciously flavored. Mr. Baihly declared that he never slaughtered a hog in this State that had any marks of disease and never one in Indiana that had not. Minnesota beef and pork are sought for in Eastern markets in preference to that raised further south.

FENCING.

It has become an established custom among farmers, in the prairie counties, to herd cattle during the summer, confining them in small yards at night. Two or three boys can thus take care of the cattle and sheep of an entire neighborhood. This obviates the necessity of fencing the fields in which grain is growing, and limits the amount of fencing required, to what is necessary for enclosing only a few acres about the houses and stabling. This saving becomes considerable, in comparison with which the cost of herding the stock is insignificant, and in the meantime the appearance of the farm is improved by the absence of unsightly fences. Where trees are planted along the highways, it takes only a few years to grow live fences, which can easily be made to turn cattle by placing poles along and nailing them to the growing trees; and for what fencing is actually needed fence-boards can be procured at low prices in every locality. Resort to these expedients greatly lessens the force of the objection urged against prairie countries, for there the expense of fencing always must be a serious consideration, especially with those who possess only small capital, if the necessity exists for fencing to protect the growing crops against cattle. It is the uniform custom throughout the State to keep hogs in enclosures of limited extent, as they give no trouble, do better and are fattened at less expense by that course of treatment.

EDUCATIONAL.

The educational facilities afforded in Minnesota, when the newness of its settlement is considered, are surprising even to those who have witnessed their gradual development, and it must severely tax the credulity of people residing elsewhere to believe half the truth. Yet the figures given below are taken from the report of the State Superintendent of Public Instruction, and there can be no doubt of their accuracy.

There are schools in seventy-one counties of the State, the number of districts being 3,811, and of school-houses 3,280. Of the latter, 2,469 are frame buildings, 136 brick, 74 stone and 601 log. The number of scholars is 167,825, and teachers employed 4,872. The average monthly wages paid teachers (including board) is $37.52 for male and $28.12 for female teachers, and the aggregate amount paid them last year was $573,-980.42. The value of school houses and sites is $3,382,351.55. The increase of scholars in 1878 over 1877 was 5,274; increase of districts 114; increase of school houses 131; increase of value of houses and sites $399,835.35; increase of teachers 130. The total cost of the schools for the year was $1,181,326.58.

The system of public schools embraces, besides the common schools, graded schools and high schools. There are seventy-eight of the former and thirty-nine or forty of the latter, and as the scholars in the lower schools advance, the number of high schools is increased, though hardly fast enough to satisfy the demand. Above the high schools and dependent upon them for its supply of scholars, is the State University, of which the Agricultural College is a department, and three excellent Normal Schools are maintained by the State for training teachers. Most munificent provision has been made for the support of public educational institutions in this State by both the general and State governments. The former donated for common schools lands equal to one-eighteenth part of the entire surveyed area of the State, and 178,086 acres additional were ceded for the University and Agricultural College. The State has pursued a sagacious policy in disposing of these so as to get the highest price for what have been sold, and the money accruing from such sales is safely invested and is already yielding a very considerable income. It is provided that no part of the principle of this sum shall be expended, but it remains a perpetual endowment for the schools, the interest only being available for current use. This greatly reduces taxation for educational purposes already, and, as its total increases every year through additional sales of land, the revenue derived from it will contribute still more largely in the future to the support of education.

Besides the public schools and higher institutions of learning, there are a large number of private and denominational schools and colleges. No statistics of these are at hand, but it is believed that they will number fully 300. While it is not strictly true that the educational facilities of the State are entirely adequate, they are equally so with those afforded even by the older States of the Union.

MISCELLANEOUS.

HEALTHFULNESS.

The healthfulness of Minnesota is best illustrated by comparisons with the rates of mortality in other countries. The total number of deaths in the State during 1877 was 6,599. This is at the rate of one in every one hundred and thirteen of the population; but 738 of these deaths were from consumption and 354 from other chronic ailments, most of which were of persons who came here invalids, too much reduced in health to recover. Deducting these and we have only one death to one hundred and thirty-five inhabitants. Lest this shall be deemed unfair, the comparison is made on the basis of charging fifty per cent. of the chronic cases to this State, when we have the following:

Minnesota	1 in 124	The whole United States.	1 in 74
Wisconsin	1 in 108	Norway	1 in 56
Iowa	1 in 93	Sweden	1 in 50
Pennsylvania	1 in 96	Denmark	1 in 46
Michigan	1 in 88	Great Britain and Ireland.	1 in 46
Illinois	1 in 73	France	1 in 41
Missouri	1 in 51	Germany	1 in 37

The chances of life in Minnesota are increased in the proportion that the above death-rates of the countries named bear to the death-rate of this State. This statement ought to remove all doubt as to the healthfulness of this climate.

WHAT WILL A HOME COST?

The question is often asked: how much money is indispensably necessary for the immigrant to bring with him to make a home in Minnesota? The answer to this depends very much upon who the questioner is, what family he has, with how little they could be content, and many other circumstances which cannot be anticipated. It is, therefore, best to tell simply *what may be done* under ordinary adventitious circumstances, in the case of a poor man going on government land.

The fees for making his claim will amount to $14, and his expenses in visiting the land office $3—total $17. The material for his house, 16x18 feet, built of single boards, covered with shingles, unplastered and having only two doors and windows, will cost $45. The work he can do himself. For winter this can be made warm enough by building a sod wall outside of the boards. Furniture, consisting of a cooking stove, crockery ware, half dozen chairs, one table and two bedsteads, will require about $40. To work his farm, a yoke of oxen $125, plow $23, wagon $75—total $223. If he begins in the spring, he can grow corn, potatoes, and garden vegetables for the first season, but will have to buy flour,—for a family of four persons, say, $30, groceries $15, cow $25, fuel $30—total $100. Add for two or three hogs, hoes, shovel, rake, scythe, and other incidentals, say $40, and we have the following:

Entry fees for land, etc.,	$17	00
Material for house,	45	00
Furniture (exclusive of bedding),	40	00
Farm implements and oxen,	223	00
Living the first 16 months,	100	00
Incidentals,	40	00
Total,	$465	00

As all his time cannot be profitably employed about his own claim, he may safely calculate upon having opportunity to work for his neighbors and earn from $100 to $150. The second spring he will require cash for seed wheat and a drag to harrow it in, say $75, and for help to harvest his grain about $75. These items added to what is given above make $612, less whatever he may earn during the year—hardly less than $100.

The second year he may confidently expect from his fifty acres of wheat 850 bushels. Deducting 200 bushels for bread and seed, and selling the remainder at 80 cents per bushel, will bring him $520. This second year his cash expenses may be limited to fuel, groceries, clothing, etc., say $200, and he has $320 to improve his house and add to his stock and farm implements. If he breaks fifty acres again this year, and secures a crop of 1,700 bushels the third year, the accomplishment of which depends mainly upon his own industry, he will be able to make himself and family comfortable and have a good home.

A single man, or even a man and wife, can do well with considerably less ready money, and so can those who have household goods, team, etc. And such as have more money than the sum given above will not be under the necessity of submitting to so many privations. Many families are living in this State and are now well off who came here with less than three hundred dollars. They, of course, depended more largely on earnings by working for their neighbors. Three things are necessary for success in any country. They are: Industry, Economy, and Careful Business Management.

TITLES TO LANDS.

The attention of readers living in Great Britain and Ireland, especially, is called to the fact that the title which a settler acquires to lands in this country is in *fee simple*. It is not a lease for any term of years, but perpetual ownership, whether he buys of the general government, State, or a railroad company The land becomes his property, to hold during life and transmit to his heirs, or he may sell it. There is no landlord, no yearly rent to pay, nor are any church rates or tithings exacted. The settler's farm is his private domain and his house is really his castle. He is himself lord of the manor and peer of his fellow-citizens of all classes. The government cannot even make a road through his premises without paying him a fair equivalent for the privilege; and all the produce he raises is his, to sell for his own benefit and that of his family. Thus he will understand that his situation must be far better than that of a tenant to ever so good a landlord, for he cannot be oppressed by increase of rental, nor evicted from his home at the whim of any human being. He becomes his own master and his own man for life, and leaves this precious legacy to his children.

MECHANICS AND LABORERS.

In all rapidly developing countries there is constant demand for skilled mechanics and intelligent laborers. Carpenters, blacksmiths, brick and stone-masons and house painters, especially, are sure of employment, and laborers who can handle axe or spade, or make a hand in the harvest field seldom remain idle. If they can also manage horses or oxen and do general farm work, they are sure of having good wages and plenty to do. Working people of these descriptions may be certain of finding equal chances of employment in Minnesota as elsewhere, if not better; and mechanics skilled in other kinds of business can form a pretty accurate estimate of the probabilities of getting employment here by reading what has been said about manufactures in the preceding pages. All sorts of manufactories here have constant demand for their wares and it must follow, therefore, that the demand for skilled laborers is regularly increasing. Minnesota shared in the general depression of business recently experienced, but not to a very severe degree, and even during its continuance there were few men in the State who could not find sufficient employment for the maintenance of themselves and families.

FISH CULTURE.

The State provided several years ago for the introduction of game fish into the lakes and streams and, under the auspices of the Commissioners, California salmon and lake salmon have been planted in a large number of the lakes, and brook trout in many of the streams. Last year the Commissioners distributed 182,850 young fish, chiefly California salmon, and kept on hand at the State fisheries 9,400 breeders, and eggs and young fry enough to make a total of 2,260,000 for distribution this season. Amongst these are 760,000 whitefish. The experiments in this line have proved eminently successful. Besides these there are vast numbers of native fish in the waters of the State, comprising several choice varieties, among which are brook trout, and fishing either for pastime or to procure food is a remunerative occupation.

IMPROVED LANDS.

It frequently happens that owners of improved farms in the older counties, desiring more land for their growing families, sell their farms at low prices and on liberal terms, and persons of means who would like to settle in Minnesota, but do not wish to go upon wild lands, will often find opportunities to purchase very desirable improved farms in good neighborhoods, and in the vicinity of the larger cities and towns.

· CATHOLIC IMMIGRATION.

The Catholic Colonization Bureau of St. Paul is doing good service in bringing immigrants into the State, and those desiring information as to its plan of operations can obtain a pamphlet, showing forth the matter very clearly, by addressing: "Secretary of Catholic Colonization Bureau, St. Paul, Minnesota."

POSTAL FACILITIES.

Every part of the State is in the enjoyment of excellent postal facilities. Daily mails are received at all the railway stations, and most localities off of these lines are served twice a week,—none less frequently than once a week. Daily papers from St. Paul are carried all over the State the same day of their publication.

HOMESTEAD EXEMPTION.

Another advantage Minnesota offers to the immigrant is the liberal law which exempts the homestead of the citizen from seizure for debt. It reads as follows:

"That a homestead consisting of any quantity of land, not exceeding eighty acres, and the dwelling-house thereon and its appurtenances, to be selected by the owner thereof, and not included in any incorporated town, city, or village, or instead thereof, at the option of the owner, a quantity of land not exceeding in amount one lot, being within an incorporated town, city or village, and the dwelling-house thereon, and its appurtenances, owned and occupied by any resident of this State, shall not be subject to attachment, levy or sale, upon any execution or any other process issuing out of any court within this State. This section shall be deemed and construed to exempt such homestead in the manner aforesaid during the time it shall be occupied by the widow or minor child or children of any deceased person who was, when living, entitled to the benefits of this act."

The same law also exempts such personal property as the Bible, pictures, school books, musical instruments, church pew, cemetery lot, wearing apparel, beds, stoves, and furniture not exceeding $500 in value; also a certain number of cows, sheep, and working team, with a year's food for the same; a wagon, sleigh, and farming implements not exceeding $100 in value; also a year's supply of family provisions, or growing crops, and seed grain not exceeding 50 bushels each of wheat and oats, 5 of potatoes and 1 of corn, also mechanics' or miners' tools, with $400 worth of stock-in-trade, and the library and implements of professional men.

It frequently happens that necessity compels one to incur debt, and no matter how well such result may be guarded against, inability to pay when the debt matures will sometimes be the condition of the most prudent and honest. Sickness, accident to person or property, or other circumstance wholly beyond the control of the individual may bring this about. Under such circumstances it is gratifying to know that the creditor cannot take from his unfortunate debtor the home, nor its furniture and conveniences, nor the food, stock, implements, tools, etc., by means of which the debtor may recover from the effect of his losses. But far greater than this is the consolation of knowing that even should death overtake one while laboring under such embarrassment, the bereaved widow and children will still be secure in the possession of their home and its comforts, and the means to gain a livelihood.

.UNOCCUPIED LANDS.

Of the unoccupied lands in Minnesota nearly 11,000,000 acres remained unsurveyed on the 1st of January, 1879. The title to these is still in the United States government, but on their survey about 600,000 acres will enure to the State as school lands, and a considerable further quantity as swamp lands and grants for railroads. Of the surveyed lands that are yet unoccupied some 3,130,000 acres still belong to the United States government, about 3,000,000 acres to the State, nearly 7,000,000 acres to railroad companies, and, perhaps, 500,000 acres to private individuals—making an aggregate of about 13,630,000 acres.

GOVERNMENT LANDS.

The lands belonging to the United States are divided among nine districts, as described hereafter, with a local land office in each for their disposal, to-wit:

1st District—Thirty miles wide across the southern part of the State, taking all of townships 101, 102, 103, 104 and 105. Office at Worthington, Mons Grinager, Register. About 10,000 acres in western counties yet to dispose of.

2d District—All of townships 106 to 110 inclusive, across the State from east to west. Office at New Ulm. C. B. Tyler, Register. About 12,000 acres in the west end not taken.

3d District—Towns 111 to 115 inclusive, across the State. Office at Redwood Falls. Wm. P. Dunnington, Register. About 10,000 acres unsold.

4th District—All of townships 116 to 120 inclusive west of the Mississippi river, and of 121 to 124 inclusive, west of range 35. Office at Benson. D. S. Hall, Register. About 65,000 acres unsold.

5th District—All of townships 125 to 136 inclusive, west of range 35. Office at Fergus Falls. Soren Listoe, Register. About 220,000 acres unclaimed.

6th District—All north of township 136 to north line of the State and west of range 35. Office at Crookston. Thomas Shapleigh, Register. About 180,000 acres unsold.

7th District—All between the St. Croix and Mississippi rivers south of where the latter is crossed by range 26, and thence northwardly, all east of range 26 and the east boundary of the State to township 46. Office at Taylor's Falls. J. P. Owens, Register. About 330,000 acres not taken.

8th District.—All north of township 45 and east of range 26 to the north and east State boundaries. Office at Duluth. R. C. Mitchell, Register. Some 1,800,000 acres not disposed of.

9th District—All between ranges 35 and 25 and north of township 120 to the British line. Office at St. Cloud. J. D. Freeman, Register. About 490,000 acres to dispose of yet.

HOW TO OBTAIN THEM.

Possession of government lands may be acquired by purchase at public or private sale, by pre-emption and subsequent purchase, or by continued occupation under the homestead and timber culture laws. The price for agricultural lands is uniformly *one dollar and twenty-five cents per acre* when beyond the limits of a railroad grant, or *two and a half dollars per acre* when within such limits. Mineral lands have their values fixed by appraisal.

When public sales of government lands are to be made, notice is given by advertisement and the lands are offered at auction to the highest bidders. To purchase at private sale the buyer goes to the land office of the district, describes the tract, and pays the full amount of purchase money.

To pre-empt land that has been offered at public sale, any person, man or woman, over twenty-one years of age, who is, or has declared his intention to become a citizen of the United States, must, within thirty days after his settlement upon the land, file a statement at the local land office of the district, declaring his intention to pre-empt such land (not more than 160 acres being allowed to one person,) and pay a fee of two dollars. Within one year of his settlement upon the land, he must make proof of his actual settlement upon and cultivation of the tract and secure the same by making payment at the prices given above. In case the land has not been offered he has three months' time in which to file his declaratory statement and thirty months before making final payment. In case a pre-emptor dies during the interval between settlement and payment, his heirs may consummate the purchase.

To obtain a homestead, (the limit being now 160 acres, whether within or outside of a railroad grant,) the applicant, either man or woman, must file his application describing the land at the local land office, together with an affidavit that he is, or has declared his intention to become a citizen, and that he desires the land for his own occupancy and for that of his family. He must then pay a commission of fourteen dollars. Having resided upon and cultivated a reasonable portion of the land continuously for five years, he must then, or within two years thereafter, prove such occupation to the district land officers and pay a further commission of *four dollars*, when he will obtain a complete title. In case of death, acquisition of title may be consummated by his heirs.

Under the Timber Culture act, the party files an application for the land and an affidavit that it is for his own use, paying *fourteen dollars*. The first year he must plow one-thirty-second part, cultivate it the second year and plant it in trees (not less than 2,700 to the acre) the third year. The second year he must plow another thirty-second part, cultivate it the third year and plant it in trees the fourth year, 2,700 to the acre. Eight years after filing application, upon proving that there are at least 675 thrifty trees on each acre on a sixteenth part of the tract, he becomes entitled to the land on payment of a further sum of four dollars. In case of death, heirs can obtain the title.

STATE LANDS.

These are scattered all over the surveyed portions of the State. Their lowest price is fixed by law at $5 per acre; and they are also separately appraised. They are always sold at public sale to the highest bidder, fifteen per cent. of the purchase money being required in cash and the remainder to draw seven per cent. per year interest until date fixed for payment at time of sale.

The railroad lands will be described in subsequent pages, to be added in the regular edition of this pamphlet.

RAILROAD LANDS.

The following descriptions of the lands of the respective railroad companies named therein, and statements of prices at and terms upon which they are offered for sale, are furnished by the companies. They have, however, been carefully reviewed, and what is said about the location, surroundings, fertility, etc., of the lands, may be relied upon as fair and unexaggerated representations. Parties desiring further information than is contained in these notices, have their attention called to the name and address of the land commissioner of the company, with which each notice closes. These officers will furnish whatever further information is wanted respecting the lands of their companies to all who apply to them. The prices are uniformly low and terms favorable to purchasers, for the companies are alive to the fact that their interests will be best subserved by the early settlement and cultivation of their lands, as they will thus secure a speedy increase of the business of their roads.

THE ST. PAUL & SIOUX CITY AND SIOUX CITY & ST. PAUL RAILROAD COMPANIES

Are offering for sale 1,000,000 acres of the choicest northwestern farming land. They are situated in the *wheat garden* and *Indian corn region* of Southwestern Minnesota and Northwestern Iowa; and are particularly desirable because of the diversity of their productions, being located in the counties of Watonwan, Martin, Cottonwood, Jackson, Murray, Nobles, Pipestone, and Rock, in Minnesota, and Lyon, Osceola, Dickinson, Sioux and O'Brien, in Iowa.

For location, soil, climate, and nearness to market, they are unequalleled. They produce per acre 20 to 40 bushels of wheat, and 40 to 60 bushels of Indian corn, and are unsurpassed for all small grain and vegetables. The soil is a deep, rich, warm loam ; lakes and streams abound, and natural " blue joint " meadows are found in every locality. There is no better stock country in the United States, and it has the most healthy climate in the world. It is too far north for fever and ague and malarious diseases, and yet not so far as to be confined to the production of wheat only. Churches, schools, mills, and thrifty towns and villages are established. Special inducements offered to settlers. Half fare excursion tickets to land seekers. For full particulars address JAMES II. DRAKE, Land Commissioner, St. Paul; or W. S. HALL, Eastern Agent, 106 Clark street, Chicago.

3 •

SOUTHERN MINNESOTA RAILWAY COMPANY.

This company is offering for sale about 340,000 acres of the very best 'farming lands, located in the counties of Houston, Fillmore, Winona, Freeborn, Faribault, Martin, Jackson, Rock, Pipestone, and Lincoln. They are mostly undulating prairie, interspersed with innumerable lakes of clear cool water, with grassy shores and gravelly bottoms, and swarming with edible fish. Streams abound throughout this region, and several of them are of considerable size, with fall enough to furnish abundant water-power for all its future needs. Many large flouring mills are already built upon them, and on the line of the Southern Minnesota Railway, affording a sure market at all times for the great wheat yield of this section. Reference to the accompanying map, will show that all but two of the counties mentioned, are traversed by railways now in operation, with from two to five trains passing daily, and those two will possess equally good railroad facilities before the close of 1879, by the extension of the Southern Minnesota Railroad from Jackson, through Pipestone county, into Dakota. All of these lands will then be within fifteen, and most of them within ten miles of the railroad.

Nearly all the government land, and a large share of the railroad lands within the above named counties, are already occupied by settlers, one family generally to each quarter section; hence it is not, in any sense, a wild region, but the advantages of society and educational facilities are already enjoyed. The official statistics of the State, give the following as its condition of development last year:

Counties.	Farms.	Acres Cultivated.	Schools.	Scholars.
·Houston......................	1,777	103,655	94	4,238
Fillmore.......................	2,593	237,553	173	8,420
Winona	1,933	146,010	109	6,559
. Faribault......................	1,168	87,099	104	3,912
Freeborn	1,762	109,489	104	4,152
Martin	605	21,538	55	1,236
. Jackson.......................	587	21,100	31	849
Rock.........................	571	35,110	16	630
Murray.......................	257	8,350	14	336
·-Lincoln......................	257	3,393	4 •	117

Pipestone not having been organized, does not appear in the report. It is safe to say, that this entire district has gained on the above figures at least twenty per cent. since that time, as there has been, for more than a year past, and continues to be a heavy immigration flowing in, for this is commonly held to be one of the most desirable localities in the Northwest. Settlers find here stores, churches, schools, etc., already established, and at the railway stations, are markets for their produce, and cheap lumber and fuel are brought in over the railway lines in abundant quantities. In short, all the advantages of civilization are at hand, and it is not surprising that multitudes avail themselves of the opportunity to secure cheap homes with such favorable surroundings.

The quality of the land for Agriculture is not surpassed anywhere, and the abundant supply of water and excellent natural meadows, constitute this one of the best grazing districts in the world. In 1877 its average yield of wheat was nearly 20 bushels per acre, and a number of farmers reported yields from 25 to 33½ bushels per acre, of grain weighing 63 lbs. per bushel. The yield of corn throughout this section is usually above the general average of the State, and no better oats, rye, barley, potatoes, and vegetables are grown.

The excellence of this portion of the State as a grazing country attracted attention of cattle-growers several years ago, and quite a number of large herds of neat cattle and flocks of sheep are to be found in different localities throughout its extent. The generally diffused and abundant supply of good water, to which access is readily obtainable at all seasons of the year, and the extensive natural meadows of nutritious grass, affording abundant pasturage in summer and hay of superior quality for winter feed, make it peculiarly attractive for those engaged in this branch of agriculture.

For similar reasons it has been found desirable for dairy farming, which business is already carried on somewhat extensively in several neighborhoods. Ten cheese factories were in operation in the above named counties in 1877, and produced 164,322 lbs. of cheese; and the State Statistician's report for the same year, shows that 2,376,521 lbs. of butter were manufactured in them that season. When it is remembered that in most of them settlements only began to be made within a very few years, this showing is simply surprising even in a country which has developed so rapidly as the State of Minnesota.

For a prairie farm one cannot do better than locate in Southern Minnesota; and it is hardly possible to buy cheaper lands than those of this company, where so many advantages are at hand.

There are two classes of these lands, to one of which the company's title is perfected, and which it offers on the following terms:

The prices are fixed at $5 to $7 per acre, and actual settlers depositing with the company *fifty cents per acre* and agreeing to break thirty per cent. of their land by July 15th, 1879, and seed the same in grain the next season, or in lieu thereof to make substantial improvements of equal value, *will not be required to make further payment until December 1st, 1880, and interest will commence at that time.*

The payment then required will be one-quarter of the purchase money (*less the fifty cents per acre previously deposited*) and seven per cent. interest for one year in advance on the remainder.

This remainder may be divided in five installments, payable annually with seven per cent. interest.

This plan enables a settler to raise and harvest a crop before any payment is required, and before interest commences.

Special discounts will be made to parties desiring to buy for cash.

The same terms will doubtless be offered another year in case any of the lands remain unsold.

To the other class, known as the lands of the Southern Minnesota Railway Extension Company, the company's title is not yet perfected, because its road is not yet completed to the western boundary of the State, and until the lands are actually conveyed to it, it cannot give deeds to settlers. But in the very improbable event of the company's failure to acquire a title to these lands the settlers can have nothing to fear, inasmuch as the lands would, in that case, be retained by the United States government, and those who had settled upon them could secure them by entries under the homestead or pre-emption laws. In order that their settlement may not be delayed, the railroad company issues permits to parties desiring to locate upon and improve them, which entitle the holders to the lands from the company, when it secures its title from the United States, on the condition that they shall in *good faith commence improvements at once, and put under cultivation, within twelve months from the date of the permit, at least forty per cent. of the lands taken,* and shall within sixty days after receiving notice from the Land Commissioner of the Company that the company has secured title to and is ready to make a formal contract of sale or deed of the lands, make such payments as may then be due on the lands and execute contracts or notes and mortgages to secure the deferred payments as is explained in what follows.

The price fixed is from $6 to $7 per acre, according to location, and payments will, as a rule, be required at the rate of one dollar per acre per annum, with interest on deferred payments at the rate of seven per cent. per annum, payable annually, but no payment of principal or interest will be required until the company is able to convey the lands by warranty deeds.

Special credits will be given as follows: For all lands broken by the 15th day of July inst., after permit, a credit at the rate of $2.50 per acre of land broken. For all additional lands broken by the 15th day of July of the next succeeding year a credit at the rate of $1.50 per acre of the land so broken. These credits will be applied, as far as they will go, on the first payments due on the lands, principal and interest.

Right of way and the necessary additional ground for the erection of screens for protection against snow will be reserved for the Southern Minnesota Railway Extension Company.

Persons buying lands of the first class mentioned, or taking the other class under permits, are, with their wives and children, carried free over the Southern Minnesota Railway, from any point on its line, when going to settle on their lands, and *greatly reduced rates* are given on their household goods, farming implements and live stock when moving on to their lands. Parties seeking lands can procure "Land Hunters' Tickets," entitling them to a return of the fare paid on this road, in case they purchase land of the company.

Rates of fare and freight on household goods, etc., from any part of the country to any point on the line of this road, and all further information respecting the lands will be furnished on application to MARSHALL CONANT, Land Commissioner, La Crosse, Wisconsin.

JESUP, JAMES AND ROOSEVELT LANDS.

These are of the lands granted to the Southern Minnesota Railroad Company, and were conveyed by that corporation to Messrs. M. K. Jesup, D. Willis James, and James A. Roosevelt, of New York, who now offer them for sale on exceedingly advantageous terms. They comprise 100,000 acres in the counties of Houston, Freeborn, Faribault, Martin, Jackson, Murray, Rock, Pipestone, Cottonwood, Lyon, Redwood, Brown and Blue Earth, and a considerable proportion are in thickly settled neighborhoods. Except those in Pipestone and Murray counties, they are all within short distances of railways over which a number of trains pass daily, and before the close of this year those in the two counties excepted, will have the same advantage of nearness to railroads.

The description given in preceding pages of the lands of the Southern Minnesota Company will apply to these, which are for the most part located in the same counties. Those that are not in counties named in that article have the same natural characteristics and are equally. as well or better off as to advantages arising from development of the country, such as schools, churches, railroads, markets, stores, &c.

The fertility and enduring quality of the soil of this entire region, and its adaptation to the cultivation of wheat, oats, corn, barley, rye, etc., cannot be questioned. The average yield of wheat in all these counties frequently exceeds 20 bushels per acre, and skillful farmers often obtain considerably more. Oats average from 30 to 45 bushels, and the yield of corn is always large while the crop matures well.

These lands have been recently carefully examined and appraised at values varying from $4 to $10 per acre, reference being had almost wholly to their locations; only a few pieces are marked at the higher figure, because of the desirableness of the neighborhoods in which they are situated. The usual valuations are $4.50 and $5 per acre. Arrangements are now made for disposing of them on a similar plan to that pursued by the State in sales of its school lands, and they will hereafter be offered at public sale in May and October of each year by Hon. O. P. Whitcomb, State Auditor, until they are all sold.

Agents in the several counties where they are located, will afford facilities for examining and ascertaining the appraised value of each tract, and give other information required.

The lands will be sold in large or small tracts to suit purchasers. Terms of payment are 15 per cent. of purchase money cash; remainder in fifteen years, with interest at rate of 7 per cent., payable annually in advance, either in June or November. The purchaser has the option, however, of making the entire payment in cash, which will entitle him to 12½ per cent. discount; or he may pay any part of the principal before it falls due.

Apply for further information to J. C. EASTON, General Agent, Lanesboro, Minnesota.

ST. PAUL & PACIFIC RAILROAD.

This is the Pioneer Railroad of Minnesota, and embraces within its lines portions of the Upper Mississippi, the whole of the fertile Sauk Valley, the Park region of Minnesota, (the Big Woods,) the rich farming and grazing lands w est of the Big Woods and midway between the Minnesota and Mississippi Rivers, and finally the famous and unsurpassed Valley of the Red River of the North, from Breckenridge, Minnesota, to Winnipeg, Manitoba, nearly three hundred miles in length and from twenty to fifty miles in breadth.

Over its Main Line passes the commerce of Central, Western and Northwestern Minnesota, N ortheastern Dakota, Manitoba, and British America, and it is the only outlet of the Great Canada-Pacific Railway.

The Branch Line is scarcely less im portant, being the natural outlet of the Upper Mississippi, the Sauk Valley and Otter Tail Countries, with numerous large water powers, where large manufacturing interests will develop.

The fertility of this entire region, and its peculiar fitness for the production of wheat, oats, corn, rye, barley, potatoes, garden vegetables, etc.; is demonstrated beyond question. It certainly is not excelled as an agricultural district, by any country, and is equalled by few. Besides this, it has the further attractio ns of being near timber, and already in the enjoyment of comme rcial, social and educational facilities. The greater part of it is justly celebrated as a grazing country and for the advantages it affords for dairy farming.

In view of the foregoing, it is not difficult to see that no better opportunities exist for all classes and conditions of people to better themselves than are found in the country tributary to this company's lines.

Homestead lands, tree claim lands, and railroad lands, conveniently located to railroads already built and in operation, at prices to meet the wants of every class. To encourage speedy settlement and cultivation of the railroad lands, the company will discount to purchasers on their time payments, about one-half the purchase money on all lands broken up.

To the tourist, sportsman and health seeker, the pure and life-renewing atmosphere, the beautiful lakes and streams, and the wood lands offer an inviting field. Many of the streams afford splendid trout fishing, and white fish, pike, pickerel, black bass, etc., are caught in most of the lakes and larger creeks and rivers.

For particulars apply to D. A. McKinlay, Land Commissioner, St. Paul, Minn.

OTHER RAILROAD LANDS.

Besides the foregoing, the St. Paul & Duluth Railroad Company, Philip S. Harris, St. Paul, Land Commissioner; the Hastings & Dakota, Geo. E. Skinner, Faribault, Minnesota, Land Commissioner; the St. Paul, Stillwater & Taylor's Falls, F. Christensen, Minneapolis, Land Agent; the Northern Pacific, James B. Powers, St. Paul, Land Commissioner; and the Chicago & Northwestern, Chas. E. Simmons, Chicago, Ill., Land Commissioner, all have considerable quantities of excellent farming lands for sale. It was expected that they would publish descriptions thereof in these pages, but they have thought proper not to do so. This determination is especially regretted for the reason that, by doing otherwise than they have, they would have contributed to include in the pamphlet descriptions of the several sections of the State in which their lands are located, which would have involved descriptions of all portions of its surveyed area.

The eastern part of the State, between the Mississippi and St. Croix rivers, in which the lands of the St. Paul & Duluth Company are situated, has not had public attention called to it, although it embraces considerable areas of good farming land and large bodies of hard wood timber. So, likewise, is there a fair proportion of good farming land in the northern and northeastern counties, which will no doubt be found capable of supporting a large population in future, when the more attractive and more easily subdued prairie lands are all occupied. These districts have labored under the disadvantage of rivalry with the prairie counties, but they have, notwithstanding, attracted considerable population, which is being augmented every year by an increased per centage of immigration.

CONCLUDING REMARKS.

It is a difficult matter to write a description of a territory as extensive as the State of Minnesota, that will convey to the reader a reasonably correct idea of the country, even when the space is not limited; but when it becomes necessary to condense this information into forty or less octavo pages, the task is really hard to accomplish. Many features that may appear sufficiently prominent to merit notice have necessarily to be ignored, and some which ought to be mentioned may be accidentally overlooked by reason of the vast multitude of topics presented to the mind of the writer. In preparing this work, the purpose has been only to enable the reader to determine for himself whether this State possesses those peculiar characteristics which are likely to make it a desirable place of residence, and the description of the country which it essays to convey, proceeds no farther. There was no intention to enter into details, because the space forbade; nor was it desirable to do anything of the sort, as that would involve the publication of a document altogether too voluminous for the use which this is intended to serve.

Pains have been taken to support the assertions, by evidence sufficiently convincing, that the soil of Minnesota is exceedingly fertile throughout almost its entire area; that wheat, corn, oats, rye, barley, potatoes, flax, hemp, amber sugar cane, melons, beans, peas, cabbage, lettuce, and nearly all varieties of vegetables cultivated in the middle States of the United States or in any part of Europe, except in those countries bordering on the Mediterranean sea, are grown here in equal perfection with and generally superior, both as to yield and quality, to those produced elsewhere; that apples, plums, grapes, strawberries, and nearly all varieties of small fruits are raised here in abundant quantities, and of superior quality. [It may be as well to remark in this place, that a mistake occurs on page 21, in giving the number of bushels of apples produced in the State in 1877, at 15,736 bushels. The quantity was 45,736 bushels.] The superiority of the State for raising stock and for dairy farming, etc., is also set forth and supported by statistics. All this should satisfy agriculturists that it is well adapted to the pursuit of their calling, in all its various branches.

The statistics given as to the development of its manufactures are enough to satisfy reasonable people of its adaptation to this department of industry. Is it probable, think you, that 452 flouring mills would be built in a State, the settlement of which was only begun about twenty-five years ago, unless there were cheaply available power to operate them, abundance of wheat for them to grind, and a greater than ordinary demand for the flour of their manufacture? And such development of any branch of industry becomes far more wonderful when it is considered that a large number of these mills are very extensive and of such superior construction, that they excite the astonishment of persons who visit the State from localities that have been settled for hundreds of years, and where they have mills which are deservedly boasted of, because of their capacity and architectural excellence. The multitude of saw and planing mills and other establishments for manufactures of wood, show that the power to operate them, the material to work up, and the demand for their products, must exist, otherwise they would not have been built. So, too, with the other manufactories mentioned.

The map shows that the State has commercial advantages which can hardly be excelled, and the number and extent of her railways is evidence that there are vast supplies of produce to carry hence to the markets of the world, and a demand for, and the means with which to purchase great quantities of commodities brought hither from other localities, for consumption within her borders; and that there is excellent reason for believing that all these occasions and opportunities for transportation will continue to be needed. The extension of these lines, north, west, and south, is strong testimony, moreover, that the countries lying contiguous to Minnesota, in these directions, are, or are soon likely to become, productive regions, requiring commercial facilities. Capitalists do not put money in such enterprises now-a-days, unless there is sufficient reason to believe that the investments will soon become profitable.

The existence within the State of some 5,000 lakes, covering areas respectively of from 40 to 130,000 acres, of four navigable rivers and of an infinite number of smaller rivers, creeks, brooks, etc., proves that the region is well watered, and the descent which it is necessary for most of these streams to make from the elevated table lands to the level of Lake Superior and the Mississippi River at St. Paul, corroborates the assertion that immense water-powers are diffused throughout the length and breadth of the State.

The extraordinary development of this country, the fact that its population has increased about ten-fold in twenty-one years; and the circumstance that very few persons who immigrate hither, ever leave because of dissatisfaction, show that it must be a desirable country to live in. That it is not too cold for comfort, and that it is more than ordinarily healthy, is demonstrated by the statistics presented on page 27.

Such is the country to which this pamphlet invites the attention of those proposing to emigrate, and if it shall be the means of contributing to direct their steps to a land where they may find a good home, surround themselves with the comforts and luxuries of life, and live contented and happy, it will have accomplished its mission.

☞ For further information address H. H. YOUNG, Secretary State Board of Immigration, St. Paul, Minnesota.

www.ingramcontent.com/pod-product-compliance
Lightning Source LLC
Chambersburg PA
CBHW061237260626
47172CB00003B/902